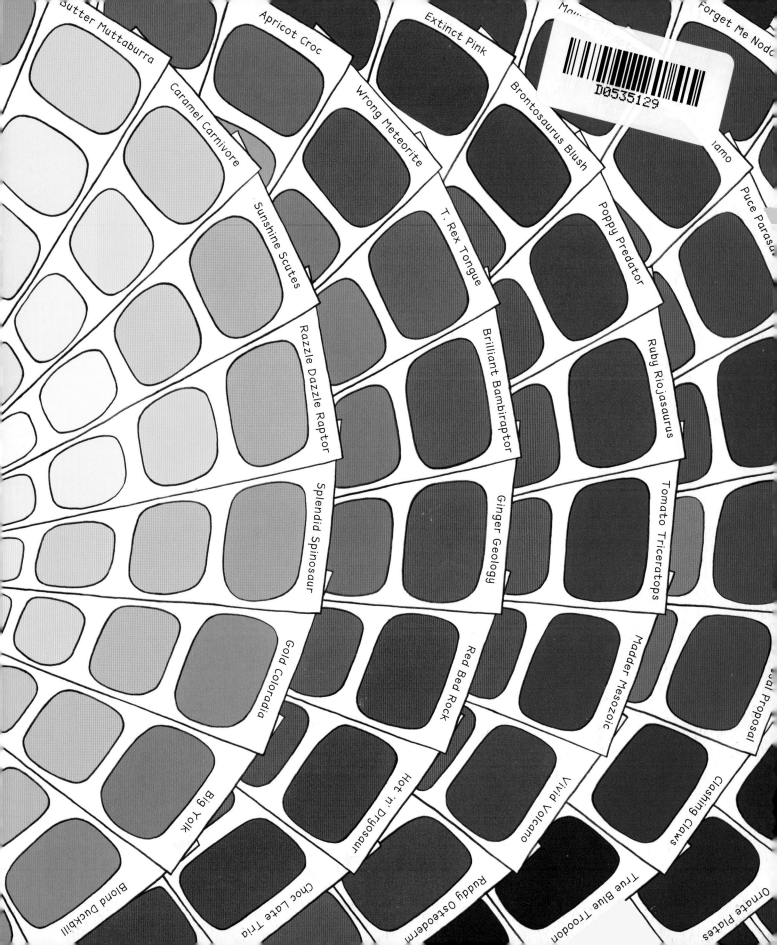

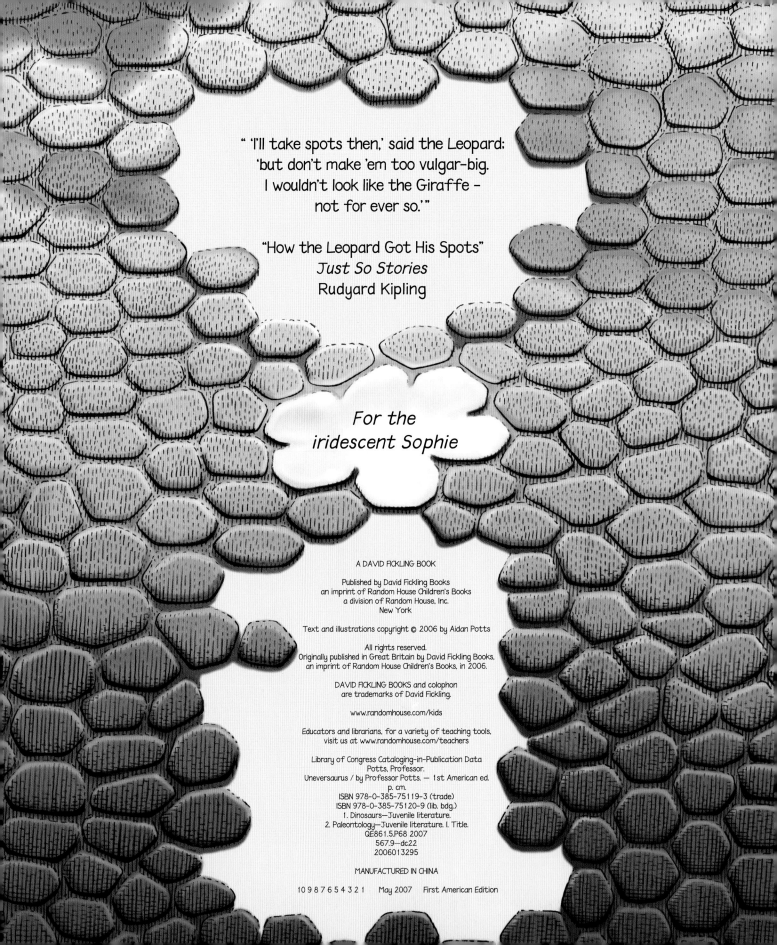

" 'I'll take spots then,' said the Leopard:
'but don't make 'em too vulgar-big.
I wouldn't look like the Giraffe -
not for ever so.' "

"How the Leopard Got His Spots"
*Just So Stories*
Rudyard Kipling

*For the
iridescent Sophie*

A DAVID FICKLING BOOK

Published by David Fickling Books
an imprint of Random House Children's Books
a division of Random House, Inc.
New York

Text and illustrations copyright © 2006 by Aidan Potts

www.randomhouse.com/kids

Educators and librarians, for a variety of teaching tools,
visit us at www.randomhouse.com/teachers

Library of Congress Cataloging-in-Publication Data
Potts, Professor.
Uneversaurus / by Professor Potts. — 1st American ed.
p. cm.
ISBN 978-0-385-75119-3 (trade)
ISBN 978-0-385-75120-9 (lib. bdg.)
1. Dinosaurs—Juvenile literature.
2. Paleontology—Juvenile literature. I. Title.
QE861.5.P68 2007
567.9—dc22
2006013295

MANUFACTURED IN CHINA

10 9 8 7 6 5 4 3 2 1     May 2007     First American Edition

Professor Potts

# UNEVERSAURUS

by
## Professor Potts

**d b** FICKLING

David Fickling Books

OXFORD · NEW YORK

# No human has ever seen a dinosaur.

SO HOW DO WE KNOW WHAT THEY LOOKED LIKE?

# Dinosaurs are buried treasure.

Their bodies have been fossilized, turned into stone. The fossils are only found in rocks that are between 65 and 230 million years old. They are worth millions of dollars.

EARLY JURASSIC TO
LATE TRIASSIC
SEDIMENTARY ROCKS

EARLY JURASSIC
BASALT

MIDDLE TO EARLY
PALEOZOIC

EARLY PALEOZOIC
AND PROTEROZOIC

PROTEROZOIC AND
MIDDLE PALEOZOIC

STRATIGRAPHIC MAP

QUATERNARY
TERTIARY
CRETACEOUS
JURASSIC
TRIASSIC
CAMBRIAN
PRECAMBRIAN

When bones are found,

they're often jumbled up.

Some bones are broken and need fixing.

Some bits are missing and need replacing.

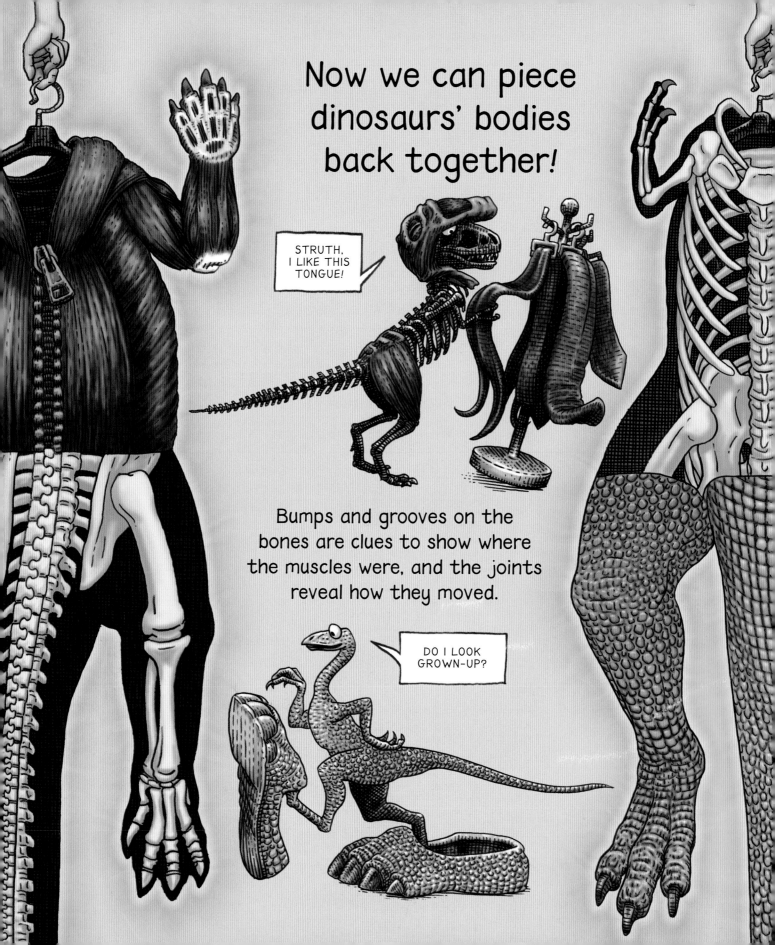

Now we can piece dinosaurs' bodies back together!

Bumps and grooves on the bones are clues to show where the muscles were, and the joints reveal how they moved.

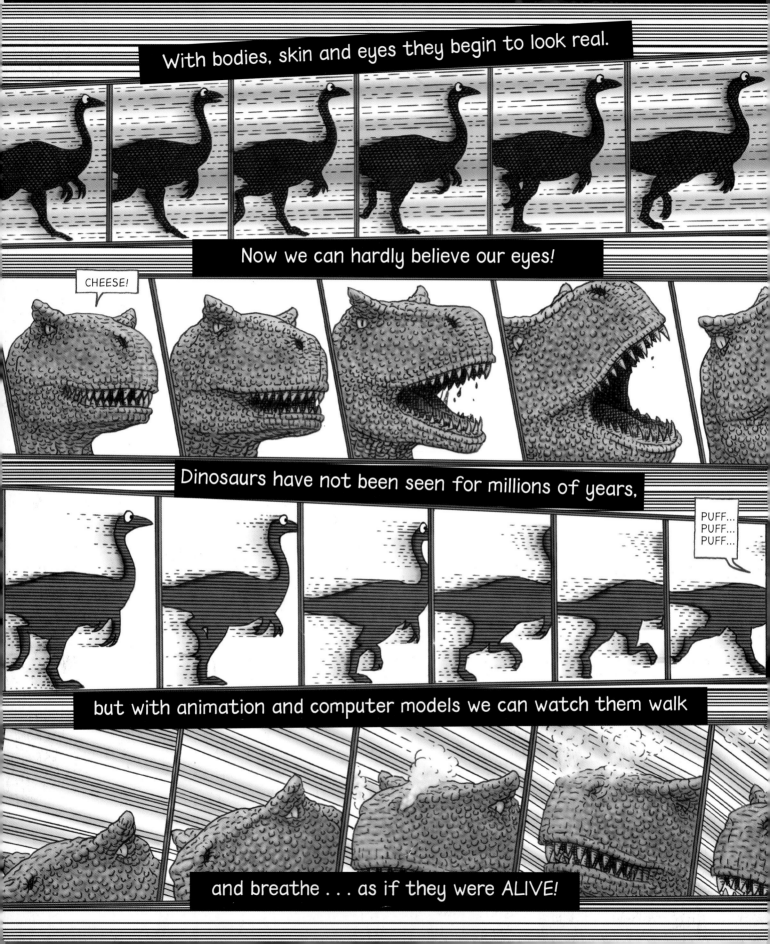

A very common type of camouflage is "countershading."

Light and shadow make things appear round, solid and easy to see.

Many creatures have a light color where there is shadow and a dark color where there is strong light.

In a way this cancels out the light from the sun.

It helps the animals to hide by looking flatter.

BERT'S SOLID GONE!

We know from plant fossils that grass was rare, so camouflage like tiger stripes wouldn't have worked.

OH NO!
I **LIKE** TIGER STRIPES.

# Hide your eyes!

Because eyes are easy to spot.

Some creatures have a dark cap or stripe.

Some reptiles can narrow their pupils into a thin slit.

U.C?    I.C!

# Some creatures are bright, bold and flashy.

They use color to surprise or scare predators. Large eyespots give a small animal a giant stare.

Color can sometimes be used as a warning. Creatures can look unappetizing. This is called aposematism.

There are so
many amazing colors
around us.

Did dinosaurs blush, just like us? It would help their bodies cool down.
It might also be a sign that said "Watch out! I'm getting A-N-G-R-Y!!!"
Red is for danger!

ADULT.

Some of today's reptiles can transform!
They change color as they grow by shedding skin.
If dinosaurs were able to do this, we need to give
them at least two different skin colors.

JUVENILE.

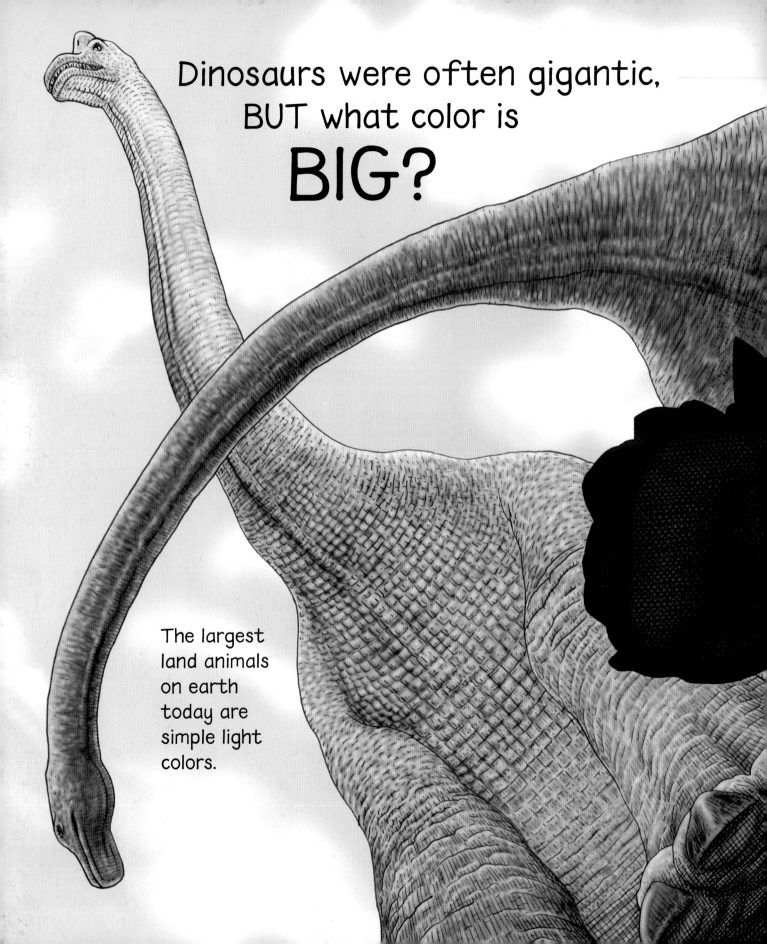

# Dinosaurs were often gigantic, BUT what color is
# BIG?

The largest land animals on earth today are simple light colors.

They have few enemies, and
they are too big to hide.
A light color helps
a big animal stay
cool inside.

ELEPHANT
HUES!

I MATCH
THE SKY!!

# Girls and boys are different.

Did Mademoiselle Dinosaur need to be dull brown to hide in her nest on the ground? Or did she wear princess pink to turn the boys' heads?

# Did boy dinosaurs prefer blue?
Did they have peacock-style displays to impress the girls?
Were they great big show-offs trying to be
the boldest and the brightest?

Reptiles and birds see more color than we do. They can see ultraviolet light. So dinosaurs might have been covered in UV markings, which human beings wouldn't be able to see.

What dinosaurs ate is important. Some animals become the same color as their food. Flamingos are **pink** because their food has a lot of red in it.

If a dinosaur ate raspberry ripple ice cream, would it become pink and white?

When I want to color a dinosaur
I close my eyes and imagine . . .
a Giganotosaur.
One of the largest-ever carnivores,
it weighed eight tons and had teeth
as sharp as a shark.

I USE
COLORS THAT
SCARE ME
OUT OF
MY SKIN!

The truth is, not even the experts know what color dinosaurs were. So we have to be creative.

THAT'S MEGA!

GIGA IS BIGGER!

# SPOT THE DINOSAUR!

Tyrannosaurus Rex

Pteranodon (flying reptiles)

Hairy Triceratops

Stegosaurus

Archaeopteryx

Sleeping Spinosaur

Gray Brachiosaurus
Brown Diplodocus

On the left: Diplodocus
On the right: Brachiosaur

Chasmosaurus

Clockwise from top center:
Corythosaurus
Tsintaosaurus
Lambeosaurus
Parasaurolophus
Saurolophus
Pachycephalosaurus

Protoceratops

Torosaurus

Carnotaurus